This edition published by Parragon Books Ltd in 2014 and distributed by

Parragon Inc.
440 Park Avenue South, 13th Floor
New York, NY 10016
www.parragon.com

ISBN 978-1-4723-5126-5

Printed in China

The BULLY
and the
Shrimp

Catherine Allison

Kim Geyer

PaRragon

Bath • New York • Cologne • Melbourne • Delhi
Hong Kong • Shenzhen • Singapore • Amsterdam

This is Noah Shrimpton.

He lives with his mom and his dad and his dog, Dixie.

He's small for his age, but he says:

Being small's not so bad!

He likes dinosaurs and superheroes and drawing in his journal.

He doesn't like carrots. Or stinky socks.

When Noah and his mom and his dad and his dog, Dixie, moved,
Noah really didn't like that very much.

He missed his friends and his old hideaway in the backyard.

"Starting at a new school's not so bad!" he told himself.

Deep down, though, he knew he was scared.

On the first day, Mom waited with him in the playground.

"They look nice," she said, pointing to a group of children nearby.

"Why don't you go over and say hello?"

But then the school bell rang, the children ran inside, and it was too late.

Noah said goodbye to his mom and went inside, too.

Mrs. Johnson, the principal, took Noah to find his classroom.

In the hall, Noah bumped into a very tall boy.

"What's your name?" asked the boy. He was wearing a T-shirt with a dinosaur on it.

"Noah Shrimpton," said Noah with a big, friendly, I'm-new-but-nice smile.

SHRIMP-BOY!

said the boy.

Noah didn't know what to think.

"Your T-shirt's cool," he said, still trying to be friendly, but his smile fading.

"I know it is," sneered the boy. "See you around, Shrimpy!"

Noah didn't know what to say.

"Connor!" said Mrs. Johnson. "We'll have none of that!"

Then she smiled at Noah. "Here we are. We'll go inside and I'll introduce you to your teacher, Mr. Preston. I'm sure you'll like him."

"Good morning, everyone," said Mr. Preston. "We have a new boy in class today—Noah Shrimpton. Let's all say hello to him."

"Hello, Noah," said the class.

"Hello, Shrimp!" shouted the boy in the dinosaur T-shirt.

Some children giggled.

"Connor, stop that!" said Mr. Preston.

"Noah, come and sit over here with Ellie and Will."

Noah felt his face turning red like a tomato.

He wanted the floor to swallow him up.

Everything was good the next day.

To start with, anyway.

And then it happened.

Noah was having his juice when Connor bumped into him. Accidentally on purpose, Noah just knew it. Juice squirted on his shirt and his pants.

Connor laughed and ran off.

Noah felt a tear begin to trickle down his cheek.

"Are you okay?" asked Ellie.

"Yes," mumbled Noah. But he didn't mean it.

After that, something bad happened every day.

Connor poured water over Noah's painting ...

... and made fun of him in class.

Connor took Noah's bag and threw it around ...

... and made faces when no one was looking.

Wherever Noah went, whatever he did, there was Connor. Being mean.

It went on ... and on ... and on ...

One recess, Ellie found Noah crying in a corner.

"Are you okay?" she asked.

"I'm fine." Noah tried to smile, but he couldn't.

"Is it Connor?" she asked.

Noah nodded. Then he told her everything. It felt good to tell her.

"Don't worry about him," Ellie said. "He's just one boy.
I'm your friend. I like you."

Noah liked Ellie, too. Just talking to her made him feel better.

But Noah didn't feel better for long.

The next morning, there was Connor in front of him.

Big and mean, with that dinosaur roaring on his T-shirt.

Noah's heart was beating so loudly he thought Connor might hear it. But he remembered Ellie saying, "I like you," and "I'm your friend," ... and a voice, a little like his own, but louder, said:

STOP!

Did I say that? thought Noah.

"What?" said Connor. He looked almost as surprised as Noah felt.

"Stop!" Noah's new, big voice said again. "Don't call me Shrimp! It's not my name."

Brrring! The school bell rang, and children rushed past to go inside.

Connor glared at Noah and ran off.

But that wasn't the end of Connor being mean.
Or of Noah using his new, big voice.

The next day, Connor elbowed Noah in the ribs and grabbed his colored pencils. "No!" said Noah, taking them back out of Connor's hands.

Then the day after, Connor pushed Noah. Hard. Noah fell backward. He was scared and red in the face, but he wasn't going to let Connor get away with it anymore.

Noah really hoped he wouldn't see Connor anymore, but there he was again when it was time to go home. Walking right up to him.

Noah's heart thumped in his chest.

"I'm sorry," Connor whispered.

"What?" said Noah.

"I'm sorry, okay?" said Connor again. "I won't do it again."

"Who was that?" asked Mom, as Connor ran off.

"Just Connor," said Noah, smiling.

So that is Noah Shrimpton.

He's small for his age, but he says, "Being small's not so bad!"

He still likes dinosaurs and superheroes and playing with his dog, Dixie.

He also likes his new school and his new friends, Ellie and Will.

And Connor—well, he's not that bad, either.

No more
Shrimp Boy!

FURTHER INFORMATION

Who are the victims of bullying?

Bullying can happen to anyone at any time. It doesn't happen because a child is weak or at fault.

What can you do if you're being bullied?

- You may find it very difficult to tell anyone what's happening, but telling someone—a parent, teacher, or friend—is the first step to making it stop. Getting a sympathetic response is a great comfort, and a bully is more likely to give up if you have someone on your side.

- Try to speak up for yourself, unless you think you are in danger physically, in which case tell an adult immediately.

- Walking away is a perfectly good way of dealing with a bully. It's nothing to be ashamed of. You don't have to listen to his or her abuse. And sometimes, standing up to a bully puts you in more danger.

- Keeping a journal can be helpful: it's a safe, private place where you can work through difficult feelings. It also forms a record of the bullying "events" that can be shared with others if necessary.

- The important thing to remember is that it's not your fault.

Developed in conjunction with educational consultants: Sandra Hall, Special Educational Needs specialist, and Mary Ann Dudko, consultant on classroom issues and concerns.